Oliver Goldsmith, Warren Fenno Gregory

Oliver Goldsmith's Traveller and Deserted Village

Oliver Goldsmith, Warren Fenno Gregory

Oliver Goldsmith's Traveller and Deserted Village

ISBN/EAN: 9783743315228

Manufactured in Europe, USA, Canada, Australia, Japa

Cover: Foto ©Andreas Hilbeck / pixelio.de

Manufactured and distributed by brebook publishing software
(www.brebook.com)

Oliver Goldsmith, Warren Fenno Gregory

Oliver Goldsmith's Traveller and Deserted Village

The Students' Series of English Classics.

OLIVER GOLDSMITH'S

TRAVELLER

AND

DESERTED VILLAGE.

" His song fresh and beautiful as when first he charmed with it."
THACKERAY.

EDITED BY

WARREN FENNO GREGORY, A.B.,

HARTFORD PUBLIC HIGH SCHOOL.

LEACH, SHEWELL, & SANBORN,
BOSTON. NEW YORK. CHICAGO.

PREFACE.

THE purpose in presenting this little volume is to lead our students to an intimate acquaintance with two poems that for more than a century and a quarter have stood with the purest, most graceful, and most pleasing productions of English literature. There must be a training of the heart as well as of the intellect; and few writings are so fitted to accomplish this as are these masterpieces, beautiful alike in thought and expression.

No true grasp of literature can be gained without a knowledge of its human side, or the author as a man. "The Traveller" and "The Deserted Village" especially demand this, as they continually reflect the feelings and experience of the poet. Goldsmith also represents a remarkable circle of men, and has an unusually pleasing and interesting personality. For these reasons an attempt has been made to provide for a careful study of his life.

So many have dealt with Goldsmith and his works, that a writer of the present day can here be but little more than "a gatherer and disposer of other men's stuff." Hence, while aiming at originality in the scope of this work, and endeavoring to secure it in treatment, the author has freely drawn his material from the accumulated mass.

WARREN FENNO GREGORY.

HARTFORD (CT.) PUBLIC HIGH SCHOOL,
November, 1894.

CONTENTS.

OLIVER GOLDSMITH.

(1728–1774.)

BIOGRAPHICAL SKETCH.

THE life of "POOR GOLDSMITH," as he has been familiarly and affectionately called, illustrates to a singular degree the force of family traits. He inherited a combination of goodness of heart, simplicity of mind, and faculty for enjoying the present in a spirit of abandon; blended with much shrewdness of observation, a rollicking Irish sense of humor, and a proverbial gift for blundering in conversation. This being the case, the conditions were right for producing one of the most helpless, thriftless, disappointing, and at the same time brilliant and lovable of all our authors.

The place of his birth is usually given as Pallas, County Longford, Ireland, the date being Nov. 10, 1728; and he was the fifth of the eight children of Charles and Ann Goldsmith. His father was at this time curate to the rector of Kilkenny West, with an income of not over £40 annually. In 1730 he succeeded his wife's uncle as rector, and settled in the pretty village of Lissoy, having now £200 a year. Little Oliver was sent to

a "dame's school" at the age of three, and impressed
the mistress as being one of the dullest boys she had
ever met with.   At six he was sent to the village school,
kept by Thomas Byrne, an old soldier who had more
fondness for fairy lore and tales of war than for the
usual branches.   Such instruction would not make an accurate scholar of a boy with his imaginative mind; but it
cultivated a poetic taste, besides filling him with a burn-
ing desire for travel and adventure.   A severe attack of
the small-pox broke off his attendance here, after which
he was sent to a better school.   His father's means
were straitened by keeping an elder son, Henry, at a
classical school; but relatives, especially his uncle, Rev.
Thomas Contarine, helped him to schools which prepared
him for the University.   His school-life was varied; on
the one hand, he was careless and dull in all studies re-
quiring steady thought, while his short, thick, ungainly
figure, his never handsome features, pitted with the
marks of disease, and his chronic blundering brought
him in among the boys for a full share of ridicule, to
which his natural sensitiveness and self-consciousness
rendered him all the more liable.   On the other hand,
his fondness for the Latin poets secured kindly attention
from his teachers, while his generous heart and fondness
for sports brought the good-will of his mates, even if
they did at times make merry at his expense.

One of many anecdotes may be introduced here.   On
his way home from his last fitting-school, supplied by
friends with a horse and a guinea, he determined to play

the man at an inn. He was sent as a joke to the house of a prominent family. These people kindly allowed the mistake to go on, so that Goldsmith swaggered through the whole performance, only to learn the true state of things next morning, to his great mortification. He afterwards used this occurrence upon which to base his comedy, " She Stoops to Conquer, or the Mistakes of a Night."

College came next; but his sister Catherine had privately married the son of a rich neighbor, and family pride prompted his father to raise a dowry of £400. This so reduced his resources that Oliver had to enter Trinity College, Dublin, as a " sizar," or poor-student, who worked in part payment of his expenses, and was distinguished by his dress. He felt the humiliation, but contrived to be merry in a happy-go-lucky way. He was fond of the flute, and played by ear with considerable sweetness. His father died in 1747, but his uncle Contarine helped him at times, and he struggled on ; sometimes writing street-ballads for sale, and again pawning his books. His nature fitted him for getting into trouble, and he was once admonished for aiding in a riot in which a bailiff was ducked and some lives lost in the attempted storming of a jail. At another time he ran away to Cork after being caned by a tutor for giving a dance in his room. He had no money to go farther; and his brother Henry arranged his return, after which he succeeded in taking the degree of B.A. in 1749.

The next thing was the choice of a profession for the

idle fellow who was living on his friends, enjoying himself at rustic merry-makings, and learning French from priests.   He was first designed for the church, and after two years of probation was rejected by the bishop.   It is said that this was for presenting himself for orders while wearing scarlet breeches.   After trying and giving up a tutorship, his relatives raised £50 for him, and with great satisfaction, no doubt, saw him mounted on a good horse, and starting for Cork to embark for America, only to have him return on a wretched beast and without a penny, having lost all in his reckless adventures.   Law was the next in order, and good uncle Contarine raised £50 more to start him as a lawyer in London.   He came back as usual, after losing his money gambling in Dublin.   The only profession left to try was that of medicine; and, supplied again with a moderate sum, he started for the medical school at Edinburgh, this time never to return.

After eighteen months of desultory work here, he wished to study abroad, and with more money from his faithful uncle he arrived in Holland after sundry misfortunes.   A fellow-countryman befriended him in Leyden, but afterwards advised him to leave, as gamblers, who were taking all he had, were getting too strong a hold on him.   He then started for Paris with his flute, a guinea, and an extra shirt.   He wandered through France and Switzerland, chiefly on foot, playing on his flute many times to secure food and lodging from the peasants.   In Italy, the land of music, this would not avail, and he is said to have taken part in disputes, or debates, at universities and convents, where the contestant would be entitled to a supper and a bed. While at Padua, where some claim that he took the degree of Bachelor of Medicine, while others say that he had previously taken it at Louvain in France, his Uncle Contarine died, and his irregular and scanty remittances of money now ceased entirely, so that he retraced his wanderings.

He arrived at Dover in 1756 in complete destitution; and while his improvidence made all his life a hard one, the next five years are peculiarly distressing, being wholly devoid of the compensations which his subsequent fame brought. He appears to have sought in vain for a place as chemist's assistant, and is said to have tried the stage, in a humble way, for a brief period. There is no definite account of his life at this time, but it is evident that he drifted towards London in a state of beggary. Here he is known to have been employed in a school, and then in a chemist's laboratory. A good Quaker physician who had been a fellow-student at Edinburgh encouraged him to practise medicine, which he did for a time in the suburbs, but unprofitably, as his patients were mainly among the poor, and could not pay him. His friend, Dr. Sleigh, helped him to a little writing for the booksellers; and a patient who was a printer for Samuel Richardson, a rich publisher and also author of "Pamela" and other novels, secured for him an introduction to his employer. Richardson gave him a little work and helped him to make some acquaintances, among whom was Dr. Young, author of "Night Thoughts." Another friend was Dr. Milner, also from Edinburgh, whose father kept a classical school, of which Goldsmith, now giving up medicine, was placed in charge during the proprietor's illness. While with the Milners he met Griffiths, a bookseller, who published the *Monthly Review*. Goldsmith was given employment on this in 1757 at a small salary, and was thus fairly started as a literary drudge. He could not long endure the exactions of the employer and his wife; and now having a little acquaintance with publishers, he shifted for himself, doing any writing that came his way. The Milners tried to befriend him again, and secured for him the appointment as post-surgeon on the coast of Coromandel. This was revoked, however; a second attempt to practise medicine proved unprofitable; he failed to pass an examination for a subordinate hospital position at the College of Surgeons, and was still in most abject poverty. Yet he was continually giving money if he had it, or even the clothes from his back and the coverings from his bed, to those who begged of him. His writings were of whatever sort would bring him money, and he had as yet produced nothing to bring him into prominence.

In 1759 he published anonymously "An Enquiry into the Present State of Polite Learning in Europe," which he had long been meditating, and in 1760 his "Chinese Letters" appeared. The money from these enabled

Goldsmith to change his wretched garret for better quarters; and, what was more, he now drew to himself valuable friends, the chief among whom was the eccentric intellectual giant, Samuel Johnson, afterwards Dr. Johnson, who was an autocrat among his literary companions, and had himself known the most grinding poverty. Goldsmith's circumstances were indeed better, but his habits still kept him in want; and Dr. Johnson told of receiving a message from him saying that he was in great distress, and begging a visit as he could not come to his friend. Dr. Johnson sent a guinea, and followed as quickly as possible to find Goldsmith under arrest in his room for arrears of rent. A fresh bottle of Madeira wine on the table showed how a portion of the guinea had already been used. Johnson promptly corked the bottle and calmed his excited friend. Upon being informed by Goldsmith that he had an unpublished manuscript by him, he at once examined it and saw its merit. He immediately sold this for £60, with which the rent was discharged, the landlady receiving an indignant lecture as well as her money. This manuscript was the copy of the "Vicar of Wakefield," published two years after.

So much of our remembrance of Goldsmith is associated with the immortal "Club" that special mention must be made of this. It was formed in 1764, and consisted of nine members who were to sup together once a week at the Turk's Head. Some of the leading ones besides our poet were Johnson, already mentioned, Joshua Reynolds, the eminent painter, Burke, the future orator, and Beauclerc, a polished aristocrat, whose appearance contrasted oddly with that of some others, but who had a fine literary taste and admired Johnson. To these were afterwards added Garrick, the actor, and Boswell, the son of a Scotch laird, who worshipped the great Johnson, sticking to him, as Goldsmith said, like a "burr," to treasure up his sayings in his memory or his note-book, and who has perpetuated the remembrance of his eminent friend and made his own otherwise insignificant name live by leaving the most complete biography ever issued. We gain much knowledge of Goldsmith from these pages, always making due allowance for the narrow-mindedness and jealousy of Boswell, who could not appreciate the poet as did the great man whom he followed.

This year, 1764, was the most important one in all Goldsmith's literary career. He had hitherto left all his writings without signature, but he now brought out the "Traveller" under his own name. The effect of this great poem on the public was immediate, bringing its author to the notice of those who had not known him, and totally changing the estimation of him in the minds of those who had. His club-mates were astounded. They had recognized ability in the man, in spite of his clumsiness in conversation, but now realized that he possessed genius, and that of the highest order. Within a year Goldsmith was called the best poet of his age. Dr. Johnson pronounced the "Traveller" the best effort in verse since the days of Pope; while the finest compliment of all came from Miss Reynolds, the sister of the painter, who said, " Well, I never more shall think Dr. Goldsmith ugly ! "

With all this success and the attendant social advantages that came with it, Goldsmith felt that he was rising in the world, and revived some of his earlier papers in a collection called " Essays by Mr. Goldsmith." He also changed lodgings again and lived with more pretension, but was still, as ever, often in want. No income could have kept pace with the way in which his generous and heedless nature would have led him to use it. He always gambled more or less, as was the fashion, and was rarely successful; but the sweeping charges of Macaulay and others on this point cannot be sustained. His disregard of expense, and habit of giving at every appeal of real or pretented distress, especially to needy countrymen of his own who flocked to him, were enough to account for the financial embarrassment which followed him, even when he came to earn perhaps £400 yearly, a large sum in those days.

In 1765, when pressed for funds, he wrote, among others, the famous nursery tale of " Goody Two Shoes," which in its own field has enjoyed as much popularity as any of his writings.

He never yet had regarded himself as permanently given up to writing; and now his increased acquaintance tempted him to the practice of medicine once more, this time in a grand way with all the gayly-colored finery of the period, but this was given up in disgust upon finding that the apothecary knew more about prescribing for a case than he did. As is so often the case, the world had settled the question of an occupation, and he never again attempted to be anything but an author.

The fame of the "Traveller" caused the "Vicar of Wakefield" to be issued after lying in the publisher's hands for two years. This added still more to his reputation, and he was now a distinguished man. Enemies had arisen, to be sure; but his social opportunities were of the best, although his natural awkwardness, never wholly to be overcome except in his writings, and his crude earlier life, placed him at a disadvantage.

He now turned his attention to another style of writing; and his comedy, "The Good-Natured Man," was produced in 1768. Its reception was disappointing in many ways. It was a sentimental age, and true comedy was not appreciated; but there was a compensation in the fact that the total profit was £500, while the "Traveller," with all its fame, brought but twenty. In a characteristic way, Goldsmith at once used the most of this money in fitting up luxurious apartments, and was really worse off than ever, as the scale of living he adopted, in the hope of continuing to earn at this rate, kept him plunged in debt for the remainder of his life.

He was now saddened by the death of his brother Henry, a careful scholar and exemplary man, who, after his university career, had abandoned thoughts of fame to settle down at Lissoy as pastor, and teacher of the

village school, " passing rich at forty pounds a year."
Oliver loved this brother with all the warmth of his
heart; and when there had been an opportunity for
patronage from the Duke of Northumberland, he had
thrown away his own chances, sturdily disclaiming all
need for himself, but mentioning his brother, and by
his natural bungling and diffidence securing nothing for
either.

We now come to an episode in Goldsmith's life which
affords the tenderest memories, and has especially ap-
pealed to Irving and Thackeray, who of all writers upon
this poet are from the gentleness of their own natures
the most truly appreciative. This is his acquaintance
with the " Jessamy Bride," a pet name applied to Miss
Mary Horneck, the younger of two beautiful daughters
of Mrs. Horneck of Devonshire. Goldsmith met this
fine family through his friend Reynolds, and formed
one of the pleasantest friendships of all his restless life.
He had at last met people of culture and position who
could understand him rightly. Goldsmith never openly
paid addresses to this lady; but Irving suspects that the
heavy tailor's charges on record for gaudy costumes
arose from a realization of his own uncouthness, and a
desire to make himself attractive in the eyes of one
he adored. There is something very touching in the
thought of a hopeless devotion, such as may have existed
here; and we well may think that had Goldsmith, with
his fine appreciation of home-life, always dear to him
and always denied, been able to win the love of such a

woman, we might now write of a longer and very different life.   It is pleasing to know that years after, the "Jessamy Bride," an aged but still charming woman, the widow of a distinguished general, paid a feeling tribute to the memory of her friend.

In 1768 the Royal Academy of Arts was instituted under the patronage of the king and the supervision of forty leading artists.   Reynolds was its president, and received the honor of knighthood, to the great delight of the Club; and the next year Johnson received from this Academy the honorary title of Professor of Ancient Literature, and Goldsmith that of Professor of Ancient History.   No salary went with this, and the recipient himself wrote to his brother Maurice that such honors were to one in his situation "something like ruffles to one wanting a shirt; " but it was a high mark of distinction, the greatest of his life.

In 1770 the "Deserted Village" appeared, bringing him one hundred guineas and additional reputation. He had now become more at ease in polite society, and we soon find him indulging in an excursion to Paris with the Hornecks, a journey which must have seemed very different from his first vagrant ramblings in France.

In 1773 he scored a triumphal success with his comedy, "She Stoops to Conquer; " and we should be glad to think of him as thoroughly happy with all these laurels, but we are forced to notice another side.   After his return from France, he had sought retirement at a farmhouse to catch up with the work, now fast getting beyond him, an all the more hopeless task because he was now often paid in advance, and the money would be spent as soon as he received it. His devotion to work here impaired his health, his pecuniary embarrassments increased, and there were never wanting envious and ill-natured critics, and those who would mortify his vanity by practical jokes at the expense of his personal appearance. As a relief from all these annoyances, he indulged in social excesses upon his return to town, with the result of further enfeebling himself. The end was coming.

He now wished to repair his fortunes by a more elaborate work than any he had yet attempted. His dream was of a dictionary of arts and sciences, for which Dr. Johnson would write on ethics, Burke on politics, Reynolds on painting, Garrick on acting, and others of note on other subjects, while Goldsmith would be editor. It was a promising undertaking if carried out, but the booksellers shrank from it. It would occupy several volumes, and they distrusted both the profit, and the prospect of completion. Then, again, work for which they had already paid would be laid aside for it. Disappointed and no longer as capable as formerly, Goldsmith settled down to forced work which was remorselessly driving him, and which was more irksome than ever. One more awakening of his former brilliancy remains in his unfinished poem, "Retaliation," inspired by mock epitaphs written for him by his companions, one of which by Garrick was especially apt, and therefore stinging : —

"Here lies poet Goldsmith, for shortness called Noll,
  Who wrote like an angel, but talked like poor Poll."

Garrick received one in return that fully repaid him, while the poet's finest effort was saved for Reynolds, for whom he had only kindness : —

" Here Reynolds is laid, and to tell you my mind,
  He has not left a wiser or better behind.
  His pencil was striking, resistless, and grand;
  His manners were gentle, complying, and bland;
  Still born to improve us in every part,
  His pencil our faces, his manners our heart.
  To coxcombs averse, yet most civilly steering,
  When they judged without skill, he was still hard of hearing;
  When they talked of their Raphaels, Correggios, and stuff,
  He shifted his trumpet, and only took snuff.
  By flattery unspoiled " ——

Goldsmith's work ended here, and worthily, with this unfinished line. He sank in a fever, and died April 4, 1774. Burke burst into tears on hearing the news, Reynolds could work no more that day, and the contemptuous amusement with which the poor fellow's social efforts had often been regarded was lost sight of in the general grief. His financial condition (he was said to be £2,000 in debt) prevented his having a public funeral, but the Club not long after placed a medallion with his likeness in Westminster Abbey, beneath which was inscribed a noble epitaph in Latin by Dr. Johnson.

As a scholar, Goldsmith was superficial and careless; as a man, we have seen him noble-hearted, but weak and erring; but as a literary artist, he remains in the front rank for his purity of thought, beauty of expression, and power to charm. In discussing his varied life, we must not make the mistake of supposing that Goldsmith stands alone. The Bohemian existence that he led was common among literary workers, and the fact that Goldsmith is often singled out as a type of irregular life among writers simply results from his being better known to us than most others of his time. We can in no wise hold his life up for imitation, while, on the other hand, there is no call to offer apologies for his errors. With his simplicity and native goodness, which no accusations on the part of those who charge him with envy can refute, his failings are more those of the child, which we regard the more kindly for its evident inability to care for itself, than those of a culprit whom we would censure. Let Goldsmith stand before us as he was, with no more excuse than his own frank nature would have sought. Irving is to be commended, who would correct Dr. Johnson's counsel : "Let not his faults be remembered, he was a very great man," by saying with a truer grasp of human nature, " Let them be remembered, since their tendency is to endear."

LITERARY PRODUCTIONS

OF

OLIVER GOLDSMITH.

"An Inquiry into the Present State of Polite Learning in Europe" (1759). His first work of importance, and published anonymously. It was severely treated by critics, and is generally considered to have little merit; but at the time it sold profitably on account of the novelty of the undertaking, and its wide range.

"The Bee" (1759). A weekly publication, of which only eight numbers were issued.

"Sketches from London" (1760). Usually spoken of as the "Chinese Letters," being a series of letters, more than a hundred in number, appearing in the *Public Ledger*, and purporting to be written by a Chinese visitor to London. A mysterious "Man in Black," who gives information to the visitor is sometimes identified with Goldsmith, and sometimes with his father, but is probably not definitely intended for either. It was Goldsmith's habit to draw characters from his own knowledge rather than from imagination, and in this way family likenesses often appear. These letters were collected next year under the title of the "Citizen of the World." Their shrewd, yet pleasant, satire upon the follies and evils of society commanded attention, and subsequent years have proven the wisdom of many of his observations and protests, which were unappreciated at the time.

"History of England" (1763). In the form of a series of letters from a nobleman to his son. A compilation of existing

16

histories, rewritten in a pleasing way. Superficial and often incorrect, but so graceful that the letters were at first thought to be those of Lord Chesterfield. It was even spoken of as "the most finished and elegant summary of English history that had ever been, or was likely to be, written."

"THE TRAVELLER, OR A PROSPECT OF SOCIETY" (1764). See introduction to this poem, p. 20.

"ESSAYS BY MR. GOLDSMITH" (1765). A collection of earlier anonymous papers made up from various periodicals.

"THE HERMIT, OR EDWIN AND ANGELINA" (1765). A shorter poem of great power and beauty published under the patronage of the Countess of Northumberland, thus having an introduction to the world which was of great advantage to Goldsmith. It was afterwards printed in the "Vicar of Wakefield." It has been called "the most finished of modern ballads."

"THE VICAR OF WAKEFIELD" (1766). A tale of domestic life in which the credulous simplicity of the good Vicar and his family, together with a childish vanity and capacity for enjoying the present, regardless of past or future, reflect many traits of the Goldsmith family. It is a story of sustained sweetness of character under misfortunes the most crushing that can come upon a man ; all eventually followed by happiness. The plot is strained and unnatural, and the incidents improbable; but it is so beautifully expressed with its simple grace and bright flashes of humor, especially in the earlier part before the clouds thicken, that it has remained one of the gems of literature. As a tale of submission in adversity with ultimate reward, it may be said to be second only to the Book of Job. Its success was immediate, and it has been greatly used and admired in France and Germany as an English text-book.

"THE GOOD–NATURED MAN" (1768). A comedy illustrating many of Goldsmith's own traits. Produced at Covent Garden with indifferent success in some respects, but a total profit of £500.

"History of the Earth and Animated Nature" (begun in 1769). This was to be a work on natural history, produced for Griffin, the bookseller, in eight volumes of 400 pages each. A hundred guineas were to be paid for the delivery of each volume in manuscript. The series was never completed. This work is interesting, but less valuable than his other writings. Facts are confused with the impossible stories of travellers, Goldsmith's credulity and lack of accurate knowledge, making him an easy dupe. At the same time, it tells in a delightful way many a pleasing thing of his own observation.

"History of Rome" (1769). Designed for students' use, and not the result of original research, but drawn from ponderous books whose contents were compiled, condensed, and rewritten in his own easy style, and thus made available for the young. In this way great service was done. Though suffering more or less from the author's carelessness and lack of thorough information, the book had so many good points that, like his "History of England," it long continued to be a standard.

"The Deserted Village" (1770). See introduction to this poem, p. 41.

"History of England" (1771). Largely a reproduction of his former one. It was well received, some critics declaring that English history had never before been "so usefully, so elegantly, and so agreeably epitomized."

"She Stoops to Conquer, or The Mistakes of a Night" (1773). A comedy based on blunders of Goldsmith's own. Its production at Covent Garden was, after a long delay, secured by the aid of Dr. Johnson, to whom the author affectionately dedicated the play when put to press. It proved very successful, bringing £800, and has lived.

"History of Greece" (1774). Prepared in the same way as his other histories.

"Retaliation" (1774). An unfinished poem, said to be his last work. See Biographical Sketch.

" A SURVEY OF EXPERIMENTAL PHILOSOPHY" (1776). A forced work under the pressure of debt, and needing no comment. As Goldsmith published nothing after 1773, the authorship of this is given on the authority of the publishers.

Besides these he left many lives of various persons, introductions to books, translations, poems, and miscellaneous articles, as he was a very prolific writer. These were mostly "hack-work,' done to procure the means of living, or of satisfying his creditors, and need no special reviewing here.

His poems were first brought out in London in two volumes, in 1780. His miscellaneous works were brought out in four volumes, in 1801, edited by S. Rose, with a memoir by Bishop Percy.

INTRODUCTION TO "THE TRAVELLER."

This poem may have in a measure been suggested by Addison's "Letters from Italy;" and the writer may have been influenced by a remark of the poet Thomson in a letter to a friend that "a poetical landscape of countries, mixed with moral observations on their characters and people, would not be an ill-judged undertaking." However this may be, the poem is peculiarly Goldsmith's own — the expression of his most sincere feelings and his personal observations; and its preparation is identified with the author's life.

The work was planned and partly composed during the author's wandering tour on the Continent, 1754–1756; and a portion of it was sent in a crude form from Switzerland to his brother Henry. It was published in 1764, and was the first work to which Goldsmith placed his name.

The plan of the poem is grand: An English wanderer seated among the peaks of the Alps looks down upon the various countries spread out before him, recalls his travels, and meditates upon the distinctive features of the lands he has examined. No one offers the complete happiness he seeks, and he comes to the conclusion that each man's feelings depend mainly upon himself, and that contentment, or its opposite, must find its causes within us, and is beyond the reach of government. While we may find it hard to accept the reasoning that opportunities for happiness are everywhere the same, we can all recognize that it is a man's privilege to be master of his mind.

Few poems have been so carefully written. It is said that the poet's spare moments during the two years previous to its publication were spent in patiently revising and retouching these lines, until the whole stands as a model of skill and taste.

It is a didactic poem in which the versifier accompanies the moralist at every step without ever losing the grace and beauty of his own especial province.

REV. HENRY GOLDSMITH.

DEAR SIR, —

I am sensible that the friendship between us can acquire no new force from the ceremonies of a dedication; and perhaps it demands an excuse thus to prefix your name to my attempts, which you decline giving with your own. But as a part of this poem was formerly written to you from Switzerland, the whole can now with propriety be inscribed only to you. It will also throw a light upon many parts of it, when the reader understands that it is addressed to a man who, despising fame and fortune, has retired early to happiness and obscurity, with an income of forty pounds a year.

I now perceive, my dear brother, the wisdom of your humble choice. You have entered upon a sacred office, where the harvest is great and the laborers are but few; while you have left the field of ambition, where the laborers are many and the harvest not worth carrying away. But of all kinds of ambition — what from the refinement of the times, from differing systems of criticism, and from the divisions of party — that which pursues poetical fame is the wildest.

Poetry makes a principal amusement among unpolished nations; but in a country verging to the extremes of refinement, painting and music come in for a share. As these offer the feeble mind a less laborious entertainment, they at first rival poetry, and at length supplant her: they engross all that favor once shown to her; and though but younger sisters, seize upon the elder's birthright.

Yet, however this art may be neglected by the powerful, it is still in greater danger from the mistaken efforts of the learned to improve it. What criticisms have we not heard of late in favor of blank verse and Pindaric odes, choruses, anapests, and iambics, alliterative care and happy negligence! Every absurdity has now a champion to defend it; and as he is generally much in the wrong, so he has always much to say — for error is ever talkative.

But there is an enemy to this art still more dangerous; I mean party. Party entirely distorts the judgment, and destroys the taste. When the mind is once infected with this disease, it can only find pleasure in what contributes to increase the distemper. Like the tiger, that seldom desists from pursuing man after having once preyed upon human flesh, the reader who has once gratified his appetite with calumny makes ever after the most agreeable feast upon murdered reputation. Such readers generally admire some half-witted thing who wants to be thought a bold man, having lost the character of a wise one. Him they dignify with the name of

poet: his tawdry lampoons are called satires; his tur-
bulence is said to be force, and his frenzy, fire.

What reception a poem may find which has neither
abuse, party, nor blank verse to support it I cannot tell;
nor am I solicitous to know. My aims are right. Without espousing the cause of any party, I have attempted
to moderate the rage of all. I have endeavoured to
show that there may be equal happiness in states that
are differently governed from our own; that every state
has a particular principle of happiness; and that this
principle in each may be carried to a mischievous excess.
There are few can judge better than yourself how far
these positions are illustrated in this poem.

   I am, DEAR SIR,

    Your most affectionate brother,

      OLIVER GOLDSMITH.

THE TRAVELLER;

OR,

A PROSPECT OF SOCIETY.

REMOTE, unfriended, melancholy, slow,
Or by the lazy Scheldt, or wandering Po;
Or onward, where the rude Carinthian boor
Against the houseless stranger shuts the door;
Or where Campania's plain forsaken lies,　　　　　5
A weary waste expanding to the skies;
Where'er I roam, whatever realms to see,
My heart untravelled fondly turns to thee;
Still to my brother turns, with ceaseless pain,
And drags at each remove a lengthening chain.　　　10
　Eternal blessings crown my earliest friend,
And round his dwelling guardian saints attend!
Blest be that spot, where cheerful guests retire
To pause from toil, and trim their evening fire:
Blest that abode, where want and pain repair,　　　15
And every stranger finds a ready chair:
Blest be those feasts with simple plenty crowned,
Where all the ruddy family around
Laugh at the jests or pranks that never fail,
Or sigh with pity at some mournful tale;　　　　　20

Or press the bashful stranger to his food,
And learn the luxury of doing good.
　But me, not destined such delights to share,
My prime of life in wandering spent and care,
Impelled with steps unceasing to pursue   25
Some fleeting good, that mocks me with the view,
That, like the circle bounding earth and skies,
Allures from far, yet, as I follow, flies,
My fortune leads to traverse realms alone,
And find no spot of all the world my own.   30
　E'en now, where Alpine solitudes ascend,
I sit me down a pensive hour to spend;
And, placed on high above the storm's career,
Look downward where an hundred realms appear —
Lakes, forests, cities, plains extending wide,   35
The pomp of kings, the shepherd's humbler pride.
　When thus creation's charms around combine,
Amidst the store should thankless pride repine?
Say, should the philosophic mind disdain
That good which makes each humbler bosom vain?   40
Let school-taught pride dissemble all it can,
These little things are great to little man;
And wiser he whose sympathetic mind
Exults in all the good of all mankind.   44
Ye glittering crowns with wealth and splendour crowned;
Ye fields where summer spreads profusion round;
Ye lakes whose vessels catch the busy gale;
Ye bending swains that dress the flowery vale;
For me your tributary stores combine:

Creation's heir, the world, the world is mine !   50
  As some lone miser, visiting his store,
Bends at his treasure, counts, recounts it o'er ;
Hoards after hoards his rising raptures fill,
Yet still he sighs, for hoards are wanting still :
Thus to my breast alternate passions rise,   55
Pleased with each good that Heaven to man supplies :
Yet oft a sigh prevails, and sorrows fall,
To see the hoard of human bliss so small ;
And oft I wish, amidst the scene, to find
Some spot to real happiness consigned,   60
Where my worn soul, each wandering hope at rest,
May gather bliss, to see my fellows blest.
  But, where to find that happiest spot below,
Who can direct, when all pretend to know ?
The shuddering tenant of the frigid zone   65
Boldly proclaims that happiest spot his own ;
Extols the treasures of his stormy seas,
And his long nights of revelry and ease ;
The naked negro, panting at the line,
Boasts of his golden sands and palmy wine,   70
Basks in the glare, or stems the tepid wave,
And thanks his gods for all the good they gave.
  Such is the patriot's boast, where'er we roam,
His first, best country, ever is at home.
And yet, perhaps, if countries we compare,   75
And estimate the blessings which they share,
Though patriots flatter, still shall wisdom find
An equal portion dealt to all mankind ;

As different good, by art or nature given,
To different nations makes their blessings even.   80
   Nature, a mother kind alike to all,
Still grants her bliss at labour's earnest call;
With food as well the peasant is supplied
On Idra's cliff as Arno's shelvy side;
And though the rocky-crested summits frown,   85
These rocks, by custom, turn to beds of down.
From art more various are the blessings sent —
Wealth, commerce, honour, liberty, content.
Yet these each other's power so strong contest,
That either seems destructive of the rest.   90
Where wealth and freedom reign, contentment fails,
And honour sinks where commerce long prevails.
Hence every state, to one loved blessing prone,
Conforms and models life to that alone.
Each to the favourite happiness attends;   95
And spurns the plan that aims at other ends;
Till, carried to excess in each domain,
This favourite good begets peculiar pain.
   But let us try these truths with closer eyes,
And trace them through the prospect as it lies: 100
Here, for a while my proper cares resigned,
Here let me sit in sorrow for mankind;
Like yon neglected shrub, at random cast,
That shades the steep, and sighs at every blast.
   Far to the right, where Apennine ascends,   105
Bright as the summer, Italy extends:
Its uplands sloping deck the mountain's side,

Woods over woods in gay theatric pride ;
While oft some temple's mouldering tops between
With venerable grandeur mark the scene.   110
   Could nature's bounty satisfy the breast,
The sons of Italy were surely blest.
Whatever fruits in different climes are found,
That proudly rise, or humbly court the ground ;
Whatever blooms in torrid tracts appear,   115
Whose bright succession decks the varied year ;
Whatever sweets salute the northern sky
With vernal lives, that blossom but to die ;
These here disporting own the kindred soil,
Nor ask luxuriance from the planter's toil ;   120
While sea-born gales their gelid wings expand
To winnow fragrance round the smiling land.
   But small the bliss that sense alone bestows,
And sensual bliss is all the nation knows.
In florid beauty groves and fields appear,   125
Man seems the only growth that dwindles here.
Contrasted faults through all his manners reign :
Though poor, luxurious ; though submissive, vain ;
Though grave, yet trifling ; zealous, yet untrue ;
And even in penance planning sins anew.   130
All evils here contaminate the mind,
That opulence departed leaves behind ;
For wealth was theirs, not far removed the date,
When commerce proudly flourished through the state ;
At her command the palace learned to rise,   135
Again the long-fallen column sought the skies,

The canvas glowed, beyond e'en nature warm,
The pregnant quarry teemed with human form;
Till, more unsteady than the southern gale,
Commerce on other shores displayed her sail; 140
While nought remained of all that riches gave,
But towns unmanned and lords without a slave:
And late the nation found with fruitless skill
Its former strength was but plethoric ill.

Yet still the loss of wealth is here supplied 145
By arts, the splendid wrecks of former pride:
From these the feeble heart and long-fallen mind
An easy compensation seem to find.
Here may be seen, in bloodless pomp arrayed,
The pasteboard triumph and the cavalcade: 150
Processions formed for piety and love,
A mistress or a saint in every grove:
By sports like these are all their cares beguiled;
The sports of children satisfy the child;
Each nobler aim, represt by long control, 155
Now sinks at last, or feebly mans the soul;
While low delights, succeeding fast behind,
In happier meanness occupy the mind:
As in those domes, where Cæsars once bore sway,
Defaced by time and tottering in decay, 160
There in the ruin heedless of the dead,
The shelter-seeking peasant builds his shed;
And, wondering man could want the larger pile,
Exalts, and owns his cottage with a smile.

My soul, turn from them, turn we to survey 165

Where rougher climes a nobler race display,
Where the bleak Swiss their stormy mansion tread,
And force a churlish soil for scanty bread;
No product here the barren hills afford
But man and steel, the soldier and his sword;   170
No vernal blooms their torpid rocks array,
But winter lingering chills the lap of May;
No zephyr fondly sues the mountain's breast,
But meteors glare, and stormy glooms invest.
    Yet still, even here, content can spread a charm,   175
Redress the clime, and all its rage disarm.
Though poor the peasant's hut, his feast though small,
He sees his little lot the lot of all;
Sees no contiguous palace rear its head,
To shame the meanness of his humble shed;   180
No costly lord the sumptuous banquet deal,
To make him loathe his vegetable meal;
But calm, and bred in ignorance and toil,
Each wish contracting, fits him to the soil.
Cheerful at morn, he wakes from short repose,   185
Breasts the keen air, and carols as he goes;
With patient angle trolls the finny deep;
Or drives his venturous ploughshare to the steep;
Or seeks the den where snow-tracks mark the way,
And drags the struggling savage into day.   190
At night returning, every labour sped,
He sits him down the monarch of a shed;
Smiles by his cheerful fire, and round surveys
His children's looks, that brighten at the blaze;

While his loved partner, boastful of her hoard,   195
Displays her cleanly platter on the board :
And haply too some pilgrim, thither led,
With many a tale repays the nightly bed.
　Thus every good his native wilds impart
Imprints the patriot passion on his heart;   200
And e'en those ills, that round his mansion rise,
Enhance the bliss his scanty fund supplies.
Dear is that shed to which his soul conforms,
And dear that hill which lifts him to the storms ;
And as a child, when scaring sounds molest,   205
Clings close and closer to the mother's breast,
So the loud torrent, and the whirlwind's roar,
But bind him to his native mountains more.
　Such are the charms to barren states assigned ;
Their wants but few, their wishes all confined.   210
Yet let them only share the praises due,
If few their wants, their pleasures are but few ;
For every want that stimulates the breast
Becomes a source of pleasure when redrest.
Whence from such lands each pleasing science flies,   215
That first excites desires, and then supplies ;
Unknown to them when sensual pleasures cloy,
To fill the languid pause with finer joy ;
Unknown those powers that raise the soul to flame,
Catch every nerve and vibrate through the frame.   220
Their level life is but a smouldering fire,
Unquenched by want, unfanned by strong desire;
Unfit for raptures, or, if raptures cheer

On some high festival of once a year,
In wild excess the vulgar breast takes fire,   225
Till, buried in debauch, the bliss expire.
    But not their joys alone thus coarsely flow :
Their morals, like their pleasures, are but low ;
For, as refinement stops, from sire to son,
Unaltered, unimproved, the manners run ;   230
And love's and friendship's finely pointed dart
Fall, blunted, from each indurated heart.
Some sterner virtues o'er the mountain's breast
May sit, like falcons cowering on the nest ;
But all the gentler morals, such as play   235
Through life's more cultured walks, and charm the way,
These, far dispersed, on timorous pinions fly,
To sport and flutter in a kinder sky.
    To kinder skies, where gentler manners reign,
I turn ; and France displays her bright domain.   240
Gay, sprightly land of mirth and social ease,
Pleased with thyself, whom all the world can please,
How often have I led thy sportive choir,
With tuneless pipe beside the murmuring Loire !
Where shading elms along the margin grew,   245
And freshened from the wave the zephyr flew ;
And haply, though my harsh touch faltering still,
But mocked all tune, and marred the dancer's skill ;
Yet would the village praise my wondrous power,
And dance, forgetful of the noontide hour.   250
Alike all ages.   Dames of ancient days
Have led their children through the mirthful maze,

And the gay grandsire, skilled in gestic lore,
Has frisked beneath the burthen of threescore.
So blest a life these thoughtless realms display ;   255
Thus idly busy rolls their world away.
Theirs are those arts that mind to mind endear,
For honour forms the social temper here ;
Honour, that praise which real merit gains,
Or even imaginary worth obtains,   260
Here passes current; paid from hand to hand,
It shifts in splendid traffic round the land :
From courts to camps, to cottages it strays,
And all are taught an avarice of praise ;
They please, are pleased, they give to get esteem,   265
Till, seeming blest, they grow to what they seem.
    But while this softer art their bliss supplies,
It gives their follies also room to rise ;
For praise too dearly loved, or warmly sought,
Enfeebles all internal strength of thought: 270
And the weak soul within itself unblest,
Leans for all pleasure on another's breast.
Hence, ostentation here, with tawdry art,
Pants for the vulgar praise which fools impart;
Here vanity assumes her pert grimace,   275
And trims her robes of frieze with copper lace ;
Here beggar pride defrauds her daily cheer,
To boast one splendid banquet once a year :
The mind still turns where shifting fashion draws,
Nor weighs the solid worth of self-applause.   280
    To men of other minds my fancy flies,

Embosomed in the deep where Holland lies.
Methinks her patient sons before me stand,
Where the broad ocean leans against the land;
And, sedulous to stop the coming tide,   285
Lift the tall rampire's artificial pride.
Onward, methinks, and diligently slow,
The firm connected bulwark seems to grow,
Spreads its long arms amidst the watery roar,
Scoops out an empire, and usurps the shore —   290
While the pent ocean, rising o'er the pile,
Sees an amphibious world beneath him smile;
The slow canal, the yellow blossomed vale,
The willow-tufted bank, the gliding sail,
The crowded mart, the cultivated plain —   295
A new creation rescued from his reign.
    Thus, while around the wave-subjected soil
Impels the native to repeated toil,
Industrious habits in each bosom reign,
And industry begets a love of gain.   300
Hence all the good from opulence that springs,
With all those ills superfluous treasure brings,
Are here displayed.   Their much-loved wealth imparts
Convenience, plenty, elegance, and arts;
But view them closer, craft and fraud appear,   305
Even liberty itself is bartered here.
At gold's superior charms all freedom flies;
The needy sell it, and the rich man buys:
A land of tyrants, and a den of slaves,
Here wretches seek dishonourable graves,   310

And, calmly bent, to servitude conform,
Dull as their lakes that slumber in the storm.
  Heavens! how unlike their Belgic sires of old —
Rough, poor, content, ungovernably bold,
War in each breast, and freedom on each brow ;   315
How much unlike the sons of Britain now !
  Fired at the sound, my genius spreads her wing,
And flies where Britain courts the western spring ;
Where lawns extend that scorn Arcadian pride,
And brighter streams than famed Hydaspes glide.   320
There, all around, the gentlest breezes stray ;
There gentlest music melts on ev'ry spray ;
Creation's mildest charms are there combined :
Extremes are only in the master's mind.
Stern o'er each bosom Reason holds her state,   325
With daring aims irregularly great.
Pride in their port, defiance in their eye,
I see the lords of human kind pass by ;
Intent on high designs, a thoughtful band,
By forms unfashioned, fresh from nature's hand,   330
Fierce in their native hardiness of soul,
True to imagined rights, above control ;
While even the peasant boasts these rights to scan,
And learns to venerate himself as man.
  Thine, Freedom, thine the blessings pictured here,   335
Thine are those charms that dazzle and endear ;
Too blest, indeed, were such without alloy,
But fostered e'en by freedom, ills annoy ;
That independence Britons prize too high,

Keeps man from man, and breaks the social tie : 340
The self-dependent lordlings stand alone,
All claims that bind and sweeten life unknown.
Here, by the bonds of nature feebly held,
Minds combat minds, repelling and repelled;
Ferments arise, imprisoned factions roar, 345
Repressed ambition struggles round her shore,
Till, overwrought, the general system feels
Its motions stopped, or frenzy fire the wheels.
  Nor this the worst. As nature's ties decay,
As duty, love, and honour fail to sway, 350
Fictitious bonds, the bonds of wealth and law,
Still gather strength, and force unwilling awe.
Hence all obedience bows to these alone,
And talent sinks, and merit weeps unknown ;
Till time may come, when, stripped of all her charms, 355
The land of scholars, and the nurse of arms,
Where noble stems transmit the patriot flame,
Where kings have toiled, and poets wrote for fame,
One sink of level avarice shall lie,
And scholars, soldiers, kings, unhonoured die. 360
  Yet, think not, thus when freedom's ills I state,
I mean to flatter kings, or court the great.
Ye powers of truth, that bid my soul aspire,
Far from my bosom drive the low desire !
And thou, fair Freedom, taught alike to feel 365
The rabble's rage, and tyrant's angry steel ;
Thou transitory flower, alike undone
By proud contempt or favour's fostering sun,

Still may thy blooms the changeful clime endure!
I only would repress them to secure;   370
For just experience tells, in ev'ry soil,
That those who think, must govern those that toil;
And all that freedom's highest aims can reach
Is but to lay proportioned loads on each.
Hence, should one order disproportioned grow,   375
Its double weight must ruin all below.
    O then how blind to all that truth requires,
Who think it freedom when a part aspires!
Calm is my soul, nor apt to rise in arms,
Except when fast approaching danger warms;   380
But, when contending chiefs blockade the throne,
Contracting regal power to stretch their own,
When I behold a factious band agree
To call it freedom when themselves are free;
Each wanton judge new penal statutes draw,   385
Laws grind the poor, and rich men rule the law;
The wealth of climes, where savage nations roam,
Pillaged from slaves to purchase slaves at home;
Fear, pity, justice, indignation start,
Tear off reserve, and bare my swelling heart;   390
Till, half a patriot half a coward grown,
I fly from petty tyrants to the throne.
    Yes, brother! curse with me that baleful hour
When first ambition struck at regal power;
And, thus polluting honour in its source,   395
Gave wealth to sway the mind with double force.
Have we not seen, round Britain's peopled shore,

Her useful sons exchanged for useless ore ?
Seen all her triumphs but destruction haste,
Like flaring tapers brightening as they waste ?   400
Seen opulence, her grandeur to maintain,
Lead stern depopulation in her train,
And over fields where scattered hamlets rose,
In barren solitary pomp repose ?
Have we not seen, at pleasure's lordly call,   405
The smiling, long-frequented village fall ?
Beheld the duteous son, the sire decayed,
The modest matron, and the blushing maid,
Forced from their homes, a melancholy train,
To traverse climes beyond the western main ;   410
Where wild Oswego spreads her swamps around,
And Niagara stuns with thundering sound ?
   Even now, perhaps, as there some pilgrim strays
Through tangled forests and through dang'rous ways,
Where beasts with man divided empire claim,   415
And the brown Indian marks with murderous aim ;
There, while above the giddy tempest flies,
And all around distressful yells arise,
The pensive exile, bending with his woe,
To stop too fearful, and too faint to go,   420
Casts a long look where England's glories shine,
And bids his bosom sympathize with mine.
   Vain, very vain my weary search to find
That bliss which only centres in the mind.
Why have I strayed from pleasure and repose,   425
To seek a good each government bestows ?

In every government, though terrors reign,
Though tyrant kings or tyrant laws restrain,
How small, of all that human hearts endure,
That part which laws or kings can cause or cure !   430
Still to ourselves in every place consigned,
Our own felicity we make or find.
With secret course, which no loud storms annoy,
Glides the smooth current of domestic joy;
The lifted axe, the agonizing wheel,   435
Luke's iron crown, and Damiens' bed of steel,
To men remote from power but rarely known,
Leave reason, faith, and conscience, all our own.

INTRODUCTION TO "THE DESERTED VILLAGE."

THIS poem, published in 1770, is the natural companion-piece of "The Traveller," which it resembles in drawing a political conclusion from a poetical description. It lacks the grandly conceived plan of the earlier poem, but is a greater general favorite, because it comes nearer the heart.

The story is of the desolate remains of a country village, which was the early home of the poet, and to which he had hoped to return, contrasted with memories of its former happy condition. Reasons are assigned for the change, and there follow general moralizings upon it, all closing in a graceful and dignified manner with "a noble address to the Genius of Poetry, in which is compressed the essence of the whole."

The "Sweet Auburn" of the poet is generally identified with Lissoy, to which Goldsmith's father removed during the infancy of his gifted son, and where Henry Goldsmith settled. It has been charged with great warmth, especially by Macaulay, that there never was such a village in Ireland, and that the poet has confused two countries; but the explanation is easy. Goldsmith composed this poem at a pleasant place in the suburbs of London where, after reaching prominence, he was accustomed to go in order to find relief from the confinement of the city. As he worked, the neatly kept hedge-rows of the soft English landscape would insensibly blend with the memories of his old home, whose harsher outlines were relieved by the glamour of early recollections, and the gathering " mist of years." It may be added that Goldsmith, while freely drawing from his own life, and the scenes of his native land, always wrote *as an Englishman.* So little doubt was there, that a Captain Hogan in a great measure restored Lissoy, to preserve local features made famous by the poet; and writers like Walter Scott and William Black are agreed that no other place could be meant.

Goldsmith had become possessed of the idea that the increase of wealth had a tendency to depopulate and lay waste the smaller villages, and affirmed that this was established by his own observation. In line with this is the allusion made near the close of " The Traveller," which leads up to this poem : —

> " Have we not seen, at pleasure's lordly call,
> The smiling, long-frequented village fall ?
> Beheld the duteous son, the sire decayed,
> The modest matron, and the blushing maid,
> Forced from their homes, a melancholy train,
> To traverse climes beyond the western main ? "

His reasoning has been sharply attacked as contrary
to the principles of political economy, and he no doubt
wrongly accounted for the changes wrought by emigration. Again, he perhaps allowed special instances that
he may have known, such as Black mentions of a village removed at the whim of an English landlord, to
stand for a general truth. It is also said by some that
Lord Robert Napier partially depopulated Lissoy by
evicting three good families with all their tenants in
order to fit up his estate as he wished. The report of
this might be enough to account for the views taken
in the poem. But it is not worth while to be critical;
a poet has the right to form his own conceptions and
adapt his material. Moreover, it is an emphatically
sound idea that happy homes are a nation's strength,
while a contented and prosperous producing class is the
true basis of society.

As this poem is the one by which most readers will
form their estimate of Goldsmith as a writer of verse,
a few general remarks upon his poetry will be in order.
The first thing to be noticed is the inconspicuousness of
his style. The matter is of more importance to him
than the manner; and at the same time his ear for music,
and familiar acquaintance with good models have enabled him to go on without jarring the reader's ear with
crude or false lines. Figures of speech are introduced
in sufficient variety, but always from well-understood
sources, and never expressed in such a way as to cause
any effort in following them or their application. We

are not challenged to stop and admire new and glittering constructions, nor ingeniously improvised words. Common speech affords the most of his material; and thus his lines pass again into common speech, and enrich the thought of thousands who are unaffected by the more ambitious masters of verse. He is strikingly free from foreign airs, uses no metrical variations caught from the Continent, and yet, by skilfully varying his pauses, avoids monotony throughout. He has a poet's mastery of epithet. Without startling us by unusual coinage, he arouses pathos by "the rattling terrors of the vengeful snake," the "matted woods," and the "intolerable day." He understands contrasts, and, what is more, knows how to harmonize their effect. We are led from the "ravaged landscape" to the "grassy-vested green," but never lose the continuity of thought. Goldsmith requires no elaborate course of learning to understand his allusions, nor trained perception to comprehend his thought. He charms all ages by his simple and tasteful use of nature; and, as Dr. Aikin says, "if this be not the highest department of poetry, it has the advantage of being the most universally agreeable."

"The Deserted Village" deserves our careful attention from the deep feeling in its thought, the music in its lines, and its entire freedom from affectation. It stands for itself, a graceful example of true English literature.

SIR JOSHUA REYNOLDS

DEAR SIR, —

I can have no expectations, in an address of this kind, either to add to your reputation or to establish my own. You can gain nothing from my admiration, as I am ignorant of that art in which you are said to excel; and I may lose much by the severity of your judgment, as few have a juster taste in poetry than you. Setting interest therefore aside, to which I never paid much attention, I must be indulged at present in following my affections. The only dedication I ever made was to my brother, because I loved him better than most other men. He is since dead. Permit me to inscribe this poem to you.

How far you may be pleased with the versification and mere mechanical parts of this attempt, I do not pretend to inquire; but I know you will object — and indeed several of our best and wisest friends concur in the opinion — that the depopulation it deplores is nowhere to be seen, and the disorders it laments are only to be found in the poet's own imagination. To this I scarce make any other answer than that I sincerely believe what I have written; that I have taken all possible pains in my country excursions for these four or five years past to be certain of what I allege ; and that all my views and inquiries have led me to believe those miseries real which I here attempt to display. But this is not the place to enter into an inquiry whether the country be depopulating or not; the discussion would take up much room, and I should prove myself, at best, an indifferent politician to tire the reader with a long preface, when I want his unfatigued attention to a long poem.

In regretting the depopulation of the country, I inveigh against the increase of our luxuries ; and here, also, I expect the shout of modern politicians against me. For twenty or thirty years past it has been the fashion to consider luxury as one of the greatest national advantages ; and all the wisdom of antiquity, in that particular, as erroneous. Still, however, I must remain a professed ancient on that head, and continue to think those luxuries prejudicial to states, by which so many vices are introduced, and so many kingdoms have been undone. Indeed, so much has been poured out of late on the other side of the question, that merely for the sake of novelty and variety one would sometimes wish to be in the right.

I am, Dear Sir,

Your sincere friend and ardent admirer,

OLIVER GOLDSMITH.

THE DESERTED VILLAGE.

SWEET AUBURN! loveliest village of the plain,
Where health and plenty cheered the labouring swain,
Where smiling spring its earliest visit paid,
And parting summer's lingering blooms delayed:
Dear lovely bowers of innocence and ease,   5
Seats of my youth, when every sport could please,
How often have I loitered o'er thy green,
Where humble happiness endeared each scene!
How often have I paused on every charm,
The sheltered cot, the cultivated farm,   10
The never-failing brook, the busy mill,
The decent church that topt the neighbouring hill,
The hawthorn bush, with seats beneath the shade,
For. talking age and whispering lovers made!
How often have I blest the coming day,   15
When toil remitting lent its turn to play,
And all the village train, from labour free,
Led up their sports beneath the spreading tree,
While many a pastime circled in the shade,
The young contending as the old surveyed;   20
And many a gambol frolicked o'er the ground,
And sleights of art and feats of strength went round:

And still, as each repeated pleasure tired,
Succeeding sports the mirthful band inspired;
The dancing pair that simply sought renown   25
By holding out to tire each other down;
The swain mistrustless of his smutted face,
While secret laughter tittered round the place;
The bashful virgin's sidelong looks of love,
The matron's glance that would those looks reprove.   30
These were thy charms, sweet village! sports like these,
With sweet succession, taught even toil to please;
These round thy bowers their cheerful influence shed;
These were thy charms — but all these charms are fled.

   Sweet smiling village, loveliest of the lawn,   35
Thy sports are fled, and all thy charms withdrawn;
Amidst thy bowers the tyrant's hand is seen,
And desolation saddens all thy green:
One only master grasps the whole domain,
And half a tillage stints thy smiling plain.   40
No more thy glassy brook reflects the day,   .
But choked with sedges, works its weedy way;
Along thy glades, a solitary guest,
The hollow-sounding bittern guards its nest;
Amidst thy desert walks the lapwing flies,   45
And tires their echoes with unvaried cries.
Sunk are thy bowers in shapeless ruin all,
And the long grass o'ertops the mouldering wall;
And, trembling, shrinking from the spoiler's hand,
Far, far away, thy children leave the land.   50

   Ill fares the land, to hastening ills a prey,

Where wealth accumulates, and men decay :
Princes and lords may flourish, or may fade —
A breath can make them, as a breath has made :
But a bold peasantry, their country's pride,   55
When once destroyed, can never be supplied.

A time there was, ere England's griefs began,
When every rood of ground maintained its man ;
For him light labour spread her wholesome store,
Just gave what life required, but gave no more :   60
His best companions, innocence and health,
And his best riches ignorance of wealth.

But times are altered ; trade's unfeeling train
Usurp the land, and dispossess the swain :
Along the lawn, where scattered hamlets rose,   65
Unwieldy wealth and cumbrous pomp repose ;
And every want to luxury allied,
And every pang that folly pays to pride.
Those gentle hours that plenty bade to bloom,
Those calm desires that asked but little room,   70
Those healthful sports that graced the peaceful scene,
Lived in each look, and brightened all the green
These, far departing, seek a kinder shore,
And rural mirth and manners are no more.

Sweet Auburn ! parent of the blissful hour,   75
Thy glades forlorn confess the tyrant's power.
Here, as I take my solitary rounds,
Amidst thy tangling walks and ruined grounds,
And, many a year elapsed, return to view
Where once the cottage stood, the hawthorn grew,   80

Remembrance wakes with all her busy train,
Swells at my breast, and turns the past to pain.
'   In all my wand'rings round this world of care,
In all my griefs — and God has given my share —
I still had hopes, my latest hours to crown,   85
Amidst these humble bowers to lay me down;
To husband out life's taper at the close,
And keep the flame from wasting by repose.
I still had hopes, for pride attends us still,
Amidst the swains to show my book-learned skill,   90
Around my fire an evening group to draw,
And tell of all I felt, and all I saw;
And, as an hare, whom hounds and horns pursue,
Pants to the place from whence at first he flew,
I still had hopes, my long vexations past,   95
Here to return — and die at home at last.
    O blest retirement, friend to life's decline,
Retreats from care, that never must be mine,
How blest is he who crowns, in shades like these,
A youth of labour with an age of ease;   100
Who quits a world where strong temptations try,
And, since 'tis hard to combat, learns to fly!
For him no wretches, born to work and weep,
Explore the mine, or tempt the dangerous deep;
Nor surly porter stands, in guilty state,   105
To turn imploring famine from the gate;
But on he moves to meet his latter end,
Angels around befriending virtue's friend;
Sinks to the grave with unperceived decay,

While resignation gently slopes the way;   110
And, all his prospects brightening to the last,
His heaven commences, ere the world be past!
   Sweet was the sound, when oft at evening's close
Up yonder hill the village murmur rose;
There, as I passed with careless steps and slow,   115
The mingling notes came softened from below;
The swain responsive as the milk-maid sung,
The sober herd that lowed to meet their young;
The noisy geese that gabbled o'er the pool,
The playful children just let loose from school;   120
The watch-dog's voice that bayed the whispering wind,
And the loud laugh that spoke the vacant mind;
These all in sweet confusion sought the shade,
And filled each pause the nightingale had made;
But now the sounds of population fail,   125
No cheerful murmurs fluctuate in the gale,
No busy steps the grass-grown footway tread,
For all the blooming flush of life is fled.
All but yon widowed, solitary thing,
That feebly bends beside the plashy spring;   130
She, wretched matron — forced in age, for bread,
To strip the brook with mantling cresses spread,
To pick her wintry faggot from the thorn,
To seek her nightly shed, and weep till morn —
She only left of all the harmless train,   135
The sad historian of the pensive plain!
Near yonder copse, where once the garden smiled,
And still where many a garden flower grows wild;

There, where a few torn shrubs the place disclose,
The village preacher's modest mansion rose.   140
A man he was to all the country dear,
And passing rich with forty pounds a year;
Remote from towns he ran his godly race,
Nor e'er had changed, nor wished to change his place;
Unpractised he to fawn, or seek for power,   145
By doctrines fashioned to the varying hour;
Far other aims his heart had learned to prize,
More skilled to raise the wretched than to rise.
His house was known to all the vagrant train,
He chid their wanderings, but relieved their pain;   150
The long-remembered beggar was his guest,
Whose beard descending swept his aged breast;
The ruined spendthrift, now no longer proud,
Claimed kindred there, and had his claims allowed;
The broken soldier, kindly bade to stay,   155
Sat by his fire, and talked the night away,
Wept o'er his wounds, or, tales of sorrow done,
Shouldered his crutch and showed how fields were won.
Pleased with his guests, the good man learned to glow,
And quite forgot their vices in their woe;   160
Careless their merits or their faults to scan,
His pity gave ere charity began.
    Thus to relieve the wretched was his pride,
And e'en his failings leaned to virtue's side;
But in his duty, prompt at every call,   165
He watched and wept, he prayed and felt for all;
And, as a bird each fond endearment tries

To tempt its new-fledged offspring to the skies,
He tried each art, reproved each dull delay,
Allured to brighter worlds, and led the way.   170
    Beside the bed where parting life was laid,
And sorrow, guilt, and pain, by turns dismayed,
The reverend champion stood.   At his control
Despair and anguish fled the struggling soul;
Comfort came down the trembling wretch to raise,   175
And his last faltering accents whispered praise.
    At church, with meek and unaffected grace,
His looks adorned the venerable place;
Truth from his lips prevailed with double sway,
And fools, who came to scoff, remained to pray.   180
The service past, around the pious man,
With ready zeal, each honest rustic ran;
E'en children followed, with endearing wile,
And plucked his gown, to share the good man's smile:
His ready smile a parent's warmth expressed,   185
Their welfare pleased him, and their cares distressed;
To them his heart, his love, his griefs were given,
But all his serious thoughts had rest in heaven.
As some tall cliff that lifts its awful form,
Swells from the vale, and midway leaves the storm,   190
Though round its breast the rolling clouds are spread,
Eternal sunshine settles on its head.
    Beside yon straggling fence that skirts the way
With blossomed furze unprofitably gay —
There, in his noisy mansion, skilled to rule,   195
The village master taught his little school;

A man severe he was, and stern to view,
I knew him well, and every truant knew;
Well had the boding tremblers learned to trace
The day's disasters in his morning face;   200
Full well they laughed with counterfeited glee
At all his jokes, for many a joke had he;
Full well the busy whisper, circling round,
Conveyed the dismal tidings when he frowned;
Yet he was kind, or if severe in aught,   205
The love he bore to learning was in fault.
The village all declared how much he knew;
'Twas certain he could write, and cipher too:
Lands he could measure, terms and tides presage,
And even the story ran that he could gauge.   210
In arguing, too, the parson owned his skill,
For e'en though vanquished, he could argue still;
While words of learnèd length and thund'ring sound
Amazed the gazing rustics ranged around,
And still they gazed, and still the wonder grew   215
That one small head should carry all he knew.
But past is all his fame. The very spot,
Where many a time he triumphed, is forgot.
  Near yonder thorn that lifts its head on high,
Where once the sign-post caught the passing eye,   220
Low lies that house where nut-brown draughts inspired,
Where gray-beard mirth and smiling toil retired,
Where village statesmen talked with looks profound,
And news much older than their ale went round.
Imagination fondly stoops to trace   225

The parlour splendours of that festive place;
The white-washed wall, the nicely sanded floor,
The varnished clock that clicked behind the door;
The chest contrived a double debt to pay,
A bed by night, a chest of drawers by day;   230
The pictures placed for ornament and use,
The twelve good rules, the royal game of goose;
The hearth, except when winter chilled the day,
With aspen boughs, and flowers and fennel gay;
While broken tea-cups, wisely kept for show,   235
Ranged o'er the chimney, glistened in a row.
   Vain transitory splendours! could not all
Reprieve the tottering mansion from its fall?
Obscure it sinks, nor shall it more impart
An hour's importance to the poor man's heart;   240
Thither no more the peasant shall repair
To sweet oblivion of his daily care;
No more the farmer's news, the barber's tale,
No more the woodman's ballad shall prevail;
No more the smith his dusky brow shall clear,   245
Relax his ponderous strength and lean to hear;
The host himself no longer shall be found
Careful to see the mantling bliss go round;
Nor the coy maid, half-willing to be pressed,
Shall kiss the cup to pass it to the rest.   250
   Yes! let the rich deride, the proud disdain,
These simple blessings of the lowly train,
To me more dear, congenial to my heart,
One native charm, than all the gloss of art;

Spontaneous joys, where nature has its play,   255
The soul adopts, and owns their first-born sway:
Lightly they frolic o'er the vacant mind,
Unenvied, unmolested, unconfined.
But the long pomp, the midnight masquerade,.
With all the freaks of wanton wealth arrayed,   260
In these, ere triflers half their wish obtain,
The toiling pleasure sickens into pain;
And, even while fashion's brightest arts decoy,
The heart distrusting asks, if this be joy?
   Ye friends to truth, ye statesmen who survey   265
The rich man's power increase, the poor's decay,
'Tis yours to judge how wide the limits stand
Between a splendid and a happy land.
Proud swells the tide with loads of freighted ore,
And shouting Folly hails them from her shore;   270
Hoards even beyond the miser's wish abound,
And rich men flock from all the world around.
Yet count our gains.   This wealth is but a name
That leaves our useful products still the same.
Not so the loss.   The man of wealth and pride   275
Takes up a place that many poor supplied;
Space for his lake, his park's extended bounds,
Space for his horses, equipage, and hounds;
The robe that wraps his limbs in silken sloth
Has robbed the neighbouring fields of half their growth;
His seat where solitary spots are seen,   281
Indignant spurns the cottage from the green;
Around the world each needful product flies,

For all the luxuries the world supplies :
While thus the land, adorned for pleasure, all   285
In barren splendour feebly waits the fall.

   As some fair female, unadorned and plain,
Secure to please while youth confirms her reign,
Slights every borrowed charm that dress supplies,
Nor shares with art the triumph of her eyes ;   290
But when those charms are past, for charms are frail,
When time advances, and when lovers fail,
She then shines forth, solicitous to bless,
In all the glaring impotence of dress ;
Thus fares the land, by luxury betrayed :   295
In nature's simplest charms at first arrayed,
But verging to decline, its splendours rise,
Its vistas strike, its palaces surprise ;
While, scourged by famine, from the smiling land
The mournful peasant leads his humble band ;   300
And while he sinks, without one arm to save,
The country blooms — a garden and a grave.

   Where then, ah ! where shall poverty reside,
To 'scape the pressure of contiguous pride ?
If to some common's fenceless limits strayed   305
He drives his flocks to pick the scanty blade,
Those fenceless fields the sons of wealth divide,
And e'en the bare-worn common is denied.

   If to the city sped — what waits him there ?
To see profusion that he must not share ;   310
To see ten thousand baneful arts combined
To pamper luxury and thin mankind ;

To see each joy the sons of pleasure know,
Extorted from his fellow-creature's woe;
Here, while the courtier glitters in brocade,   315
There, the pale artist plies the sickly trade;
Here, while the proud their long-drawn pomps display,
There, the black gibbet glooms beside the way.
The dome where pleasure holds her midnight reign,
Here, richly decked, admits the gorgeous train;   320
Tumultuous grandeur crowds the blazing square,
The rattling chariots clash, the torches glare.
Sure scenes like these no troubles e'er annoy;
Sure these denote one universal joy!
Are these thy serious thoughts? — Ah! turn thine
        eyes   325
Where the poor houseless shivering female lies.
She once, perhaps, in village plenty blessed,
Has wept at tales of innocence distressed;
Her modest looks the cottage might adorn,
Sweet as the primrose peeps beneath the thorn;   330
Now lost to all; her friends, her virtue fled,–
Near her betrayer's door she lays her head —
And, pinched with cold, and shrinking from the shower,
With heavy heart deplores that luckless hour,
When idly first, ambitious of the town,   335
She left her wheel and robes of country brown.
    Do thine, sweet Auburn! thine the loveliest train,
Do thy fair tribes participate her pain?
E'en now, perhaps, by cold and hunger led,
At proud men's doors they ask a little bread.   340

Ah, no ! To distant climes, a dreary scene,
Where half the convex world intrudes between,
Through torrid tracts with fainting steps they go,
Where wild Altama murmurs to their woe.
Far different there from all that charmed before,   345
The various terrors of that horrid shore;
Those blazing suns that dart a downward ray,
And fiercely shed intolerable day;
Those matted woods where birds forget to sing;
But silent bats in drowsy clusters cling;   350
Those poisonous fields with rank luxuriance crowned,
Where the dark scorpion gathers death around;
Where at each step the stranger fears to wake
The rattling terrors of the vengeful snake;
Where crouching tigers wait their hapless prey,   355
And savage men more murderous still than they;
While oft in whirls the mad tornado flies,
Mingling the ravaged landscape with the skies.
Far different these from every former scene,
The cooling brook, the grassy-vested green,   360
The breezy covert of the warbling grove,
That only sheltered thefts of harmless love.
  Good Heaven! what sorrows gloomed that parting
    day,
That called them from their native walks away;
When the poor exiles, every pleasure past,   365
Hung round the bowers, and fondly looked their
    last —
And took a long farewell, and wished in vain

For seats like these beyond the western main —
And, shuddering still to face the distant deep,
Returned and wept, and still returned to weep. 370
The good old sire the first prepared to go
To new-found worlds, and wept for others' woe;
But for himself, in conscious virtue brave,
He only wished for worlds beyond the grave.
His lovely daughter, lovelier in her tears, 375
The fond companion of his helpless years,
Silent went next, neglectful of her charms,
And left a lover's for a father's arms.
With louder plaints the mother spoke her woes,
And blessed the cot where every pleasure rose, 380
And kissed her thoughtless babes with many a tear,
And clasped them close, in sorrow doubly dear;
Whilst her fond husband strove to lend relief
In all the silent manliness of grief.

   O luxury! thou curst by Heaven's decree, 385
How ill exchanged are things like these for thee!
How do thy potions, with insidious joy,
Diffuse their pleasures only to destroy!
Kingdoms, by thee to sickly greatness grown,
Boast of a florid vigour not their own: 390
At every draught more large and large they grow,
A bloated mass of rank unwieldy woe;
Till, sapped their strength, and every part unsound,
Down, down they sink, and spread a ruin round.

   Even now the devastation is begun, 395
And half the business of destruction done;

Even now, methinks, as pondering here I stand,
I see the rural virtues leave the land.
Down where yon anchoring vessel spreads the sail
That idly waiting flaps with every gale,   400
Downward they move, a melancholy band,
Pass from the shore, and darken all the strand.
Contented toil, and hospitable care,
And kind connubial tenderness are there,
And piety with wishes placed above,   405
And steady loyalty, and faithful love.
And thou, sweet Poetry, thou loveliest maid,
Still first to fly where sensual joys invade;
Unfit, in these degenerate times of shame,
To catch the heart, or strike for honest fame: 410
Dear charming nymph, neglected and decried,
My shame in crowds, my solitary pride;
Thou source of all my bliss, and all my woe,
Thou found'st me poor at first, and keep'st me so;
Thou guide, by which the noble arts excel,   415
Thou nurse of every virtue, fare thee well!
Farewell; and oh! where'er thy voice be tried,
On Torno's cliffs, or Pambamarca's side,
Whether where equinoctial fervours glow,
Or winter wraps the polar world in snow,   420
Still let thy voice, prevailing over time,
Redress the rigours of the inclement clime;
Aid slighted truth with thy persuasive strain;
Teach erring man to spurn the rage of gain;
Teach him, that states of native strength possessed,   425

Though very poor, may still be very blest;
That trade's proud empire hastes to swift decay,
As ocean sweeps the laboured mole away;
While self-dependent power can time defy,
As rocks resist the billows and the sky.   430

INTRODUCTION TO NOTES.

THE thought in the Spanish proverb, that the view of a forest may be obscured by calling attention to the trees, has been borne in mind in preparing these notes. They are arranged with the design of securing an appreciation of these poems, rather than making an exhaustive study of word-derivation and grammatical points, though such matters are not neglected when deemed necessary to bring out the meaning. It is not considered advisable to enable the student to dispense with his dictionary, nor to dwell upon points that should have been instilled at an earlier period. When the time is reached at which this book is expected to be used in schools, the literary spirit should not be surrendered too much to the pedagogic.

In class-work, it is suggested that the accompanying outlines be followed. They can be elaborated with minor points according to the amount of time to be given to each poem. Then if each student takes a portion of the syllabus to speak upon, the result will be a satisfaction to all, as the writer can testify from his own work. The memorizing of choice portions is of the greatest value, and should be much employed here, as these poems are so well fitted for it. Finally, each one should read them carefully, with no other thought than that of enjoyment; and if this be not fully secured, there is something wrong. The essence of literature is that it must entertain; poetry is its highest form, and these are among the best specimens of poetry.

If these poems are read with the author's own feeling in mind, that "innocently to amuse the imagination in this dream of life is wisdom," they will achieve their true and kindly purpose, and linger delightfully in the memory.

NOTES ON THE TRAVELLER.

STRUCTURE OF THE POEM. — Both these poems are written in iambic pentameter, often called *heroic verse;* a metrical form which is to the English, German, and Italian Languages what the hexameter is to Greek and Latin. Ruskin says: "The tetrameter and pentameter, which require the full breath, but do not exhaust it, constitute the entire body of the chief poetry of energetic nations; the hexameter, which fully exhausts the breath, is only used by nations whose pleasure was in repose." Iambic pentameter is scanned thus: —

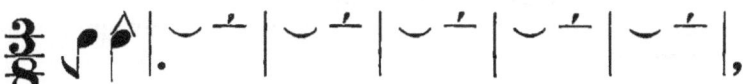

"Where'ér | I roám, ‖ whatév- | er lańds | to sée,
My heárt ‖ untráv- | elled fońd- | ly tufns | to thée."
The Traveller.

" The háw- | thorn búsh, ‖ with scáts | beneáth | the sháde,
For tálk- | ing áge ‖ and whís- | pering lóv- | ers máde."
The Deserted Village.

The cæsura, or natural pause, indicated thus ‖, which is needed in most lines longer than the tetrameter verse, may in this form come anywhere in the line, but is found most frequently after the fourth or sixth syllable.

The lines are arranged in rhymed couplets, a system fully developed in the polished verse of Pope. The rules governing this were that there should be a pause, a comma at least, at the end of every couplet, and no sentence should close except with the end of a line. An extra syllable was guarded against. Such couplets lend themselves readily to quotation, and hence live in our language; but the artificial nature of the whole arrangement caused poets, later on, to turn to more varying and less mechanical forms.

65

Outline of the Poem.

Lines 1-22. **A tender address** to the poet's brother Henry, in his quiet and useful life.

23-30. **The Poet's** own restless and wandering condition is placed in contrast.

31-50. **The panorama** of a "hundred realms," seen from the Alpine summits, invites consideration.

51-62. **A wish** for a spot of real happiness.

63-72. **The claim** by the dweller in each region that his own home is best.

73-98. **The patriot's boast** is called in question.

99-104. **A proposition** is made to try the truth by observation of different countries.

105-164. **Italy** is surveyed and discussed.

165-238. **Switzerland** and her people receive attention.

239-280. **France,** with her people, passes in review.

281-316. **Holland** is examined in the same manner, and also fails to satisfy.

317-334. **Britain** is taken under consideration.

335-422. **A discussion** of freedom, suggested by the proud independence of the British character, and the abuses that arise even from this.

423-438. **The conclusion** is reached that happiness centres in the mind, independent of location or government, and is not to be gained by travelling in search of it.

Page 25, Line 1. **Remote, etc.** Cf. Ovid's "Metam.," xiv. 217: —

"Solus, inops, exspes: leto poenisque relictis."
Hopeless, unaided, alone; the pains of death now await him.

P. 25, l. 1. **Slow.** It is said that a fellow-member of the Club asked: "Mr. Goldsmith, what do you mean by the last word in the first line of your 'Traveller'? Do you mean tardiness of locomotion?" Goldsmith, who habitually spoke unthinkingly, answered, "Yes." Dr. Johnson, the autocrat of the company, who was sitting near, at once broke out with, " No, sir; you did not mean tardiness of locomotion; you mean that sluggishness of mind that comes upon a man in solitude." — " Ah! " said Goldsmith, abashed, " *that* was what

I meant." Instances like this gave rise to the charge that Johnson largely aided in the preparation of the poem, when, in fact, he contributed but nine lines, of inferior quality compared with Goldsmith's own.

P. 25, l. 2. **Scheldt, Po.** The Scheldt flows from France through Belgium and Holland to the North Sea. The Po is the largest river of Italy, flowing from west to east across the upper part to the Adriatic Sea. Thus these two rivers represent the extreme points of the travels described.

P. 25, l. 3. **Carinthian.** The inhabitants of Carinthia, a mountainous province of south-western Austria, were called rough and inhospitable.

P. 25, l. 5. **Campania.** The *Campagna di Roma*, a low plain surrounding the city of Rome.

P. 25, l. 9. **My brother.** Henry Goldsmith, to whom the poem was dedicated.

P. 25, l. 10. **A lengthening chain.** Cf. Cibber's " Com. Lover," p. 249: —

"'When I am with Florimel, it [my heart] is still your prisoner, it only draws a longer chain after it.'"

P. 26, l. 23. **Me.** The object of the transitive verb *leads* in line 29.

P. 26, l. 32. **I sit me down.** This reflexive use of the personal pronoun is common in earlier English.

P. 26, l. 33. **Above the storm's career.** The poet is represented as sitting on a crag of the Alps, at an elevation above that of ordinary rain-clouds.

P. 26, l. 34. **An hundred realms.** Poetical use of the numeral. Notice, also, the use of "an" before the sounded *h*. This was always done by Goldsmith.

P. 28, l. 84. **Idra's cliff.** Probably Idria, a mining-town of Austro-Hungary.

P. 28, l. 84. **Arno's shelvy side.** The Arno, a river of Tuscany, flows through the most fertile land in Italy. Hence the thought is that there are means of livelihood for those living in the most sterile places, as well as for those in the most productive. "Shelvy" is shelving or sloping.

P. 28, l. 101. **Proper cares.** Those strictly belonging to himself. Latin *Proprius, -a, -um*, one's own.

P. 28, l. 105. **Apennine.** The Apennines; mountains running from the Alps through the Italian peninsula.

P. 29, l. 111. **Could.** Verb with *if* understood. The conclusion of the condition is the subjunctive *were*, line 112. The form is that of a Latin condition contrary to fact in present time.

P. 29, l. 123. **Small the bliss, etc.** Pleasure given by the animal senses is by the poet viewed as far below the enjoyment obtained by the intellect.

P. 29, l. 134. **When Commerce flourished.** Venice and Genoa controlled a large part of European commerce during the Middle Ages. As Italy weakened, other nations secured this.

P. 29, l. 135. **At her command, etc.** Referring to the Italian renaissance, or revival of art in the fifteenth century.

P. 30, l. 144. **Plethoric ill.** "In short, the state resembles one of those bodies bloated with disease, whose bulk is only a symptom of its wretchedness: their former opulence only rendered them more impotent." — *Citizen of the World,* i. 98.

P. 30, l. 150. **The pasteboard triumph.** Instead of the "triumph" of Roman times, when a commander entered the city in state, after a decisive victory, the mummery of the Carnival is seen.

P. 31. l. 170. **Man and steel.** In earlier times the Swiss were in great demand as hired soldiers, and often secured money for their families in this way.

P. 31, l. 186. **Breasts.** Often incorrectly given as "breathes," with a sad loss of poetic vigor.

P. 31, l. 190. **Savage.** A savage beast.

"Drive the reluctant savage into the toils." — *Citizen of the World,* i. 112.

P. 32, l. 205. **As a child, etc.** No feature of Goldsmith's poems impresses the mind more than his fine similes, of which this is a beautiful example.

P. 32, l. 213. **For every want, etc.** In a pessimistic way we may say that civilization is but an increase of wants. The brighter side of this view is here brought out. Cf. "Animated Nature," ii. 123.

"Every want becomes a means of pleasure in the redressing."

P. 32, l. 217. **Unknown to them, etc.** Poetical contraction of statement. In prose: "When sensual pleasures cloy, how to fill the languid pause with finer joy is unknown to them."

P. 33, l. 243. **Choir.** The choral dance.

P. 33, l. 249. **Yet would the village praise, etc.** The adventures of George Primrose in " The Vicar of Wakefield " are regarded as being those of Goldsmith himself, allowing for the flourishes incident to story-telling. He says: " I passed among the harmless peasants of Flanders, and among such of the French as were poor enough to be very merry; for I ever found them sprightly in proportion to their wants. Whenever I approached a peasant's house towards nightfall, I played one of my most merry tunes, and that procured me not only lodging but subsistence for the next day."

P. 34, l. 262. **From courts to camps, to cottages.** Instances of " apt alliteration's artful aid " are frequent in these poems.

P. 34, l. 280. **Self-applause.** Legitimate self-satisfaction, and not vanity or conceit.

P. 35, l. 284. **The broad ocean, etc. Cf.:**

"And view the ocean leaning on the sky." — *Dryden.*

P. 35, l. 290. **Scoops out.** A striking instance of the power of a fitly-chosen simple word to call up an entire image.

P. 35, l. 296. **A new creation, etc.**

" Holland seems to be a conquest upon the sea, and in a manner rescued from its bosom." — *Goldsmith.*

P. 35, l. 306. **Even liberty, etc.** Slavery was permitted in Holland, and children could be sold by their parents for a certain number of years.

P. 36, l. 313. **Their Belgic sires.** The time-honored expression of Cæsar's " Commentaries," " The bravest of all these are the Belgians," must have been in Goldsmith's mind.

P. 36, l. 319. **Where lawns, etc.** Goldsmith's residence in England had so far been one of squalor and wretchedness, but it is the England of beauty of which he writes. Cf. his " Citizen of the World," ii. 196: —

" Yet from the vernal softness of the air, the verdure of the fields, the transparency of the streams, and the beauty of the women; here love might sport among the painted lawns and warbling groves, and carol upon gales wafting at once both fragrance and harmony."

P. 36, l. 319. **Arcadian.** Arcadia, an exceedingly fertile state in the south of ancient Greece, is the traditional type of rural simplicity and happiness.

P. 36, l. 320. **Hydaspes.** A river of India, now called Jhylom or Jelum. On its banks Alexander the Great defeated Porus. It is celebrated by Lucan, the elder Pliny, Arrian, and other Latin writers of whose works Goldsmith was fond.

P. 37, l. 345. **Ferments arise, etc.**

"It is extremely difficult to induce a number of free beings to co-operate for their mutual benefit: every possible advantage will necessarily be sought, and every attempt to procure it must be attended with a new fermentation."
Citizen of the World, ii. 228.

Our own country is well illustrating in its social and political life the sageness of Goldsmith's views on this.point.

P. 37, l. 348. **Frenzy fire the wheels.** An infinitive phrase, the object of the verb "feels," line 347.

P. 37, l. 357. **Stems.** Offspring.

"A rod out of the stem of Jesse." — *Isa.* xi. 1.

P. 37, l. 361. **Yet think not, etc.**

"In the things I have hitherto written, I have neither allured the vanity of the great by flattery, nor satisfied the malignity of the vulgar by scandal: but have endeavored to get an honest reputation by liberal pursuits."
Preface to History of England.

P. 38, l. 382. **Contracting regal power, etc.**

"It is in the interest of the great to diminish kingly power as much as possible." — *Vicar of Wakefield,* p. 101.

P. 38, l. 392. **Petty tyrants.** Cf. Pope's "Epistle to Mrs. Blount:" —

"Marriage may all these petty tyrants chase."

P. 39, l. 405. **Have we not seen, etc.** These lines are evidently the starting-point of "The Deserted Village."

P. 39, ll. 411, 412. **Oswego . . . Niagara.** Goldsmith was the first to introduce sonorous Indian names into English poetry. It is true that the metrical accent here calls for Niagára, but other good poets have made worse slips on names belonging even to their own land.

P. 39, l. 412. **With thundering sound.** Burke had applied this epithet to the falls.

P. 39, l. 420. **This philosophical line** was contributed by Dr. Johnson.

P. 40, ll. 429–438. **These lines** are also Dr. Johnson's, with the exception of lines 435, 436. Their weighty nature shows a marked contrast to the easy flow of the rest of the poem, and the two simple lines of Goldsmith's own are worth more than all his friend's well-meant contribution.

P. 40, l. 435. **The agonizing wheel.** In France and Germany, those deemed worthy of especial punishment were sometimes bound upon wheels, which were made to revolve while the executioner broke each limb with a bar of iron as it came up.

P. 40, l. 436. **Luke's iron crown.** George and Luke Zeck, brothers, headed an insurrection in Hungary in 1514. George, who attempted to seize the sovereignty, was punished by having a red-hot iron crown placed upon his head. The name of his brother Luke is taken here, evidently for metrical reasons.

P. 40, l. 436. **Damien's bed of steel.** Robert François Damiens, for attempting to assassinate Louis XV. of France, in 1757, was kept for two months upon a heated bed of steel, in order to wring from him the names of supposed confederates. As there appeared to be none, he was finally torn limb from limb by horses. Goldsmith had, when abroad, been much moved by the tyrannical and luxurious lives of the French kings, and had shrewdly predicted: "If they have but three weak monarchs more successively on the throne, the mask will be laid aside, and the country will certainly once more be free."

NOTES ON THE DESERTED VILLAGE.

N. B. — Read the "Introduction to Notes," p. 63, and the note on poetical structure, p. 65, as these apply equally to both poems.

72

303–336. **The hopeless efforts** of outcast poverty to find a place for itself.

337–362. **The fortunes** of Auburn's exiled inhabitants.

363–384. **The sadness** of expulsion from home.

385–394. **A reproach** against luxury.

395–430. **The displacement** by luxury of the rural virtues, and with them the Genius of Poetry. To her the poet appeals that she teach erring men the truth through all time.

PAGE 47, LINE 2. **Swain.** A favorite word among eighteenth-century poets. Originally meaning a servant, it came to be used for a young man in the country, — a husbandman, as here, — a shepherd; and, from the pastoral sentiment of the times, a lover.

P. 47, l. 4. **Parting.** Departing. Cf. line 1 of Gray's "Elegy:"—

"The curfew tolls the knell of parting day."

P. 47, l. 5. **Bowers.** Poetically used for dwellings.

P. 47, l. 13. **The hawthorn bush.** A large hawthorn (hedge-thorn) bush in Lissoy was carried away piecemeal by relic-hunters.

P. 47, l. 14. **Talking age.**

"And narrative old age."— POPE.

P. 47, l. 15. **The coming day.** Some saint's day, which would be a festal occasion, celebrated on the village green.

P. 47, l. 17. **Train.** Often used by Goldsmith, and occurring some ten times in this poem; coming from the Latin *traho*, to draw, it means here a long-drawn line.

P. 47, l. 21. **Gambol.** A general joining in play.

P. 48, l. 35. **Lawn.** Equivalent to "plain" in line 1.

P. 48, l. 39. **Only.** Perhaps the hardest word in our language to use properly. Here, as an adjective, it is given an especial force by its position. Cf.:—

"Now is it Rome indeed, and room enough,
When there is in it but one only man."
Julius Cæsar, Act I. Scene ii.

P. 48, l. 42. **Works its weedy way.** A noticeable instance of the alliteration often used by Goldsmith and other poets of his time. Cf. lines 53, 74, 82, 93, 102, 123, 214, and 281 as examples. As a striking illustration which this line suggests, notice the following from Boker's "Ivory Carver:"—

> "Silently sat the artist alone,
>   Carving a Christ from the ivory bone.
>   Little by little, with toil and pain,
>   He won his way through the sightless grain,
>   That held and yet hid the thing he sought,
>   Till the work stood up, a growing thought."

P. 48, l. 44. The hollow-sounding bittern, etc. A species of heron, locally known in this country as "stake-driver," from the sound of its cry. Goldsmith, in his "Animated Nature," observes that there is "no note so dismally hollow as the booming of the bittern." The name is used in the Scriptures with melancholy suggestiveness: —

"I will also make it a possession for the bittern, and pools of water."
Isa. xiv. 23.

"But the cormorant and the bittern shall possess it; the owl also and the raven shall dwell in it." — *Ibid.* xxxiv. 11.

P. 48, l. 51. Ill fares the land, etc. Almost the only line of Goldsmith's that has been criticised as inartistic; exception being taken to the repetition of sound in "ill" and "ills."

P. 48, l. 52. Decay. Lessen in number.

P. 49, l. 55. A breath, etc. Cf.: —

"Princes and lords are but the breath of kings." — BURNS.

P. 49, l. 66. Wealth . . . pomp. Goldsmith is much addicted to this form of personification, often using a quality, condition, or occupation for those whom it represents.

P. 49, l. 70. Manners. Customs. An evident choice of words for the sake of alliteration.

P. 49, l. 75. Sweet Auburn, etc. An example of apostrophe.

P. 50, ll. 87, 88. These lines form an excellent metaphor.

P. 50, l. 93. As an hare, etc. Goldsmith, with good taste, refrains from overloading his lines with figures of speech, and when introduced they are exceedingly effective, like the simile here. For the use of "an" before the aspirated *h*, Cf. "The Traveller," line 34.

P. 50, l. 107. His latter end. Extreme old age. Cf. the biblical use: —

"Hear counsel, and receive instruction, that thou mayest be wise in thy latter end." — *Prov.* xix. 20.

P. 51, l. 110. **While resignation, etc.** Sir Joshua Reynolds, to whom this poem was dedicated, appreciated the fine tribute, and soon painted his picture of " Resignation," inscribed, " This attempt to express a character in ' The Deserted Village ' (lines 109–112) is dedicated to Dr. Goldsmith by his sincere friend and admirer, JOSHUA REYNOLDS."

P. 51, l. 121. **Bayed.** Barked at.
> " I had rather be a dog, and bay the moon,
>   Than such a Roman." — *Julius Cæsar*, Act IV., Scene iii.

P. 51, l. 121. **The whispering wind.** Wind is regularly to be pronounced *wind* in poetry.

P. 51, l. 122. **The loud laugh, etc.** Mr. Swinton makes a good point here by observing that this does not mean that *every* loud laugh betokens an empty mind.

P. 51, l. 124. **The nightingale.** Those whose delight it is to pick flaws in greatness say here that the nightingale is not found in Ireland. This is true; but, as said before, it was perfectly natural for the poet to mingle his surroundings, while writing the poem, with his recollections of childhood.

P. 51, l. 129. **Yon widowed, solitary thing.** The general absence of life in the village is made far more impressive by a special instance of its presence in a forlorn condition, as a feeble sound emphasizes a profound silence.

Pp. 51–53, ll. 137–192. **The sketch of the village preacher** seems to be drawn from the poet's father, and his brother, Henry Goldsmith, combined. The literary idea may come from the parish priest of Dryden, who, in turn, improved the character from Chaucer.

P. 51, l. 137. **Copse.** A field of brushwood which is cut for fuel. French *couper*, to cut.

P. 51, l. 138. **Still.** Adverbial modifier of " grows." Placed where it is on account of the metre.

P. 52, l. 142. **Passing.** Surpassingly. Exceedingly.

P. 52, l. 155. **Broken.** Broken down.

P. 52, l. 159. **Glow.** Become animated, with face flushed with interest.

P. 52, l. 167. **And as a bird, etc.** This beautiful simile is believed to be strictly original, having thus an advantage over the loftier one in lines 189–192. The thought may come from Deut. **xxxii.** 11, 12 ; but there is no parallel to it in poetic literature.

P. 53, l. 173. **Champion.** One who combats singly for himself or another. Here, the defender of the departing soul against the powers of evil. From the Latin *campus*, a field, hence a place for contests.

P. 53, l. 181. **The service past** = When the service was finished. Nominative absolute.

P. 53, l. 189. **As some tall cliff, etc.** No sublimer simile is to be found, and this should never leave the mind of the reader. It is probably adapted from the following passage from Young's "Night Thoughts," but gains greatly upon it : —

> " As some tall tower, or lofty mountain's brow,
> Detains the sun, illustrious from its height,
> White rising vapors and descending shades,
> With damps and darkness drown the spacious vale,
> Philander thus augustly rears his head."

Pp. 53, 54, ll. 193–216. **The character of the village schoolmaster** recalls Goldsmith's old teacher, Thomas, commonly called " Paddy " Byrne, a veteran whose tales seem to have suggested the " broken soldier " of the previous description.

P. 53, l. 194. **Furze.** An evergreen shrub, often called gorse.

P. 53, l. 195. **Skilled to rule.** A trace of Latin infinitive construction. Cf. line 145.

P. 54, l. 209. **Terms and tides presage.** Foretell seasons, and times of high and low water.

P. 54, l. 210. **Gauge.** Estimate the capacity of casks from their dimensions.

P. 54, l. 219. **Thorn.** Thorn-tree.

P. 54, l. 221. **That house.** The village inn.

P. 55, l. 232. **The twelve good rules.** These were attributed to Charles I., and were commonly hung in public-houses. They were: 1. Urge no healths [the drinking of " healths " to each other]. 2. Profane no divine ordinances. 3. Touch no state matters. 4. Reveal no secrets. 5. Pick no quarrels. 6. Make no comparisons. 7. Maintain no ill opinions. 8. Keep no bad company. 9. Encourage no vice. 10. Make no long meals. 11. Repeat no grievances. 12. Lay no wagers.

P. 55, l. 232. **The royal game of goose.** A fox-and-geese board.

P. 55, l. 234. **Fennel.** An aromatic garden plant.

P. 55, l. 244. **The Woodman's ballad.** Some song of Robin Hood, the hero of forestry.

P. 55, l. 248. **The mantling bliss.** Happiness that included or infolded all. Used by metonymy for the ale which was the cause.

P. 55, l. 250. **Shall kiss the cup, etc.** Cf. the song : —

> " Drink to me only with thine eyes,
> And I will pledge with mine ;
> Or leave a kiss but in the cup,
> And I'll not look for wine."
>
> *To Celia.* — BEN JONSON.

P. 56, l. 258. **Unenvied, unmolested, unconfined.** The prefix *un-* has elsewhere been effectively used in poetry. Cf. : —

> "Unwept, unhonored, and unsung." — SCOTT.
> " Unknelled, uncoffined, and unknown." — BYRON.

P. 56, l. 264. **The heart distrusting asks if this be joy.** One of the most powerful lines in the poem, or in our language.

P. 56, l. 278. **Equipage.** Carriages and attendants. Fr. *équiper*, to attire.

P. 57, l. 284. **For.** In exchange for.

P. 57, l. 287. **Plain.** Not meaning devoid of beauty, which would be a contradiction, but simple and modest.

P. 57, l. 293. **Solicitous to bless.** By giving her hand in marriage.

P. 57, l. 298. **Vistas.** Extended prospects. Especially applied to views through avenues of trees.

P. 58, l. 316. **Artist.** In the sense of artisan, or workman.

P. 58, l. 317. **Pomps.** Here meaning processions. From the Greek *pempo*, to send.

P. 58, l. 319. **Dome.** Here used by synecdoche for the entire palace.

P. 58, l. 322. **The torches glare.** Before the lighting of streets, people of fashion were attended in the streets at night by torch-bearers or link-boys.

P. 58, l. 330. **Sweet as the primrose peeps beneath the thorn.** So good a judge as William Black declares that the sentiment which a poetic imagination can infuse into surrounding objects never received happier expression than in this line. It truly represents that mysterious something in a combination of words which we call poetry.

P. 59, l. 344. **The wild Altama.** The Altamaha, one of the boundaries of Georgia. This colony was settled in 1732 by General Oglethorpe, whom Goldsmith knew.

P. 59, l. 355. **Crouching tigers.** Goldsmith's ideas of American natural history were somewhat mixed. By "tiger," he is here supposed to mean the jaguar, which does not make it much better, as this is a South American animal. It is possible that he may have heard of the panther.

Pp. 59, 60, ll. 363–384. **The pathos of emigration** has, perhaps, never been so effectively set forth as in these lines.

P. 60, l. 368. **Seats.** Sites, abodes.

P. 60, l. 392. **A bloated mass, etc.** Cf. his discussion of Italy, "The Traveller," line 144.

P. 61, l. 400. **Flaps.** One of the class of onomatopoetic, or sound-imitative words. From their nature they are often effective in poetry, since they call up an image to the mind, as here. Other examples of such words in this poem are "gabbled," "plashy," "clock," "murmur," etc.

P. 61, l. 411. **Dear charming nymph.** Still referring to poetry personified. The nymphs were female divinities of lesser rank than the commonly-known goddesses.

P. 61, l. 413. **Thou source, etc.** Wither's lines to his muse, in his poem of "The Shepherd's Hunting," are often quoted in comparison with this : —

> "And though for her sake I'm crost,
> Though my best hopes I have lost,
> And knew she would make me trouble,
> Ten times more than ten times double,
> I should love and keep her too
> Spite of all the world could do. . . .
> She doth tell me where to borrow
> Comfort in the midst of sorrow,
> Makes the desolatest place
> To her presence be a grace."

P. 61, l. 418. **Torno's Cliffs, or Pambamarca's side.** The river Tornea flows through a mountainous region in Sweden, and Pambamarca is a peak of the Andes in Ecuador. Thus the wish is expressed that the influence of poetry may be world-wide.

P. 61, l. 419. **Equinoctial.** Equatorial.

Pp. 61, 62, ll. 427–430. **These lines were added by Dr.** Johnson, who was nothing if not **profound, and who thought** the poem ended too tamely. His heavy lines do not well accord with the graceful flow of Goldsmith's verse, and we can but wish, as in " The Traveller," that he had saved his ponderous assistance until it was more needed. The final thought, as the author would have left it, was the natural conclusion of a poem whose surpassing sweetness has rendered its popularity independent of all changes in literary style.

Prices largely reduced.

The Students' Series of English Classics.

Carlyle's The Diamond Necklace . . . . . . 35 cts.
 Edited by W. F. MOZIER, High School, Ottawa, Ill.

Macaulay's Essays on Milton and Addison . . . . 35 "
 Edited by JAMES CHALMERS, Ohio State University.

Selections from Washington Irving . . . . . . 50 "
 Edited by ISAAC THOMAS, High School, New Haven, Conn.

Scott's Lady of the Lake . . . .
 Edited by JAMES ARTHUR TUFTS, Phillips Exeter Academy.

Selected Orations and Speeches . . . .
 Edited by C. A. WHITING, University of Utah.

Lays of Ancient Rome . . . .
 Edited by D. D. PRATT, High School, Portsmouth, Ohio.

Goldsmith's Traveller and Deserted Village . . . . 25 "
 Edited by W. F. GREGORY, High School, Hartford, Conn.

Burke's Speech on Conciliation with America . .
 Edited by L. DU PONT SYLE, University of California.

Macaulay : Life of Samuel Johnson ; Essay on Byron . .
 Edited by GAMALIEL BRADFORD, JR., Instructor in Literature,
  Wellesley and Boston.

Wordsworth's White Doe of Rylstone . . . . .
 Edited by MARY HARRIOTT NORRIS, Professor of English
  Literature.

Tennyson's Elaine . . . . 25 "
 Edited by FANNIE MORE MCCAULEY, Instructor in English
  Literature, Winchester School, Baltimore.

*All are substantially bound in cloth. The usual discount will be made
for these books in quantities.*

LEACH, SHEWELL, & SANBORN, Publishers.

BOSTON. NEW YORK. CHICAGO.